CW00500991

Clarinet
Scales & Arpeggios
from 2018
ABRSM Grades 6–8

Contents

First published in 2017 by ABRSM (Publishing) Ltd, a wholly owned subsidiary of ABRSM
© 2017 by The Associated Board of the Royal Schools of Music
Unauthorized photocopying is illegal

Music origination by Julia Bovee
Cover by Kate Benjamin & Andy Potts
Printed in England by Halstan & Co. Ltd, Amersham, Bucks., on materials from sustainable sources
P14785

Grade 6

SCALES

from memory
tongued *and* slurred

two octaves   ♩ = 96

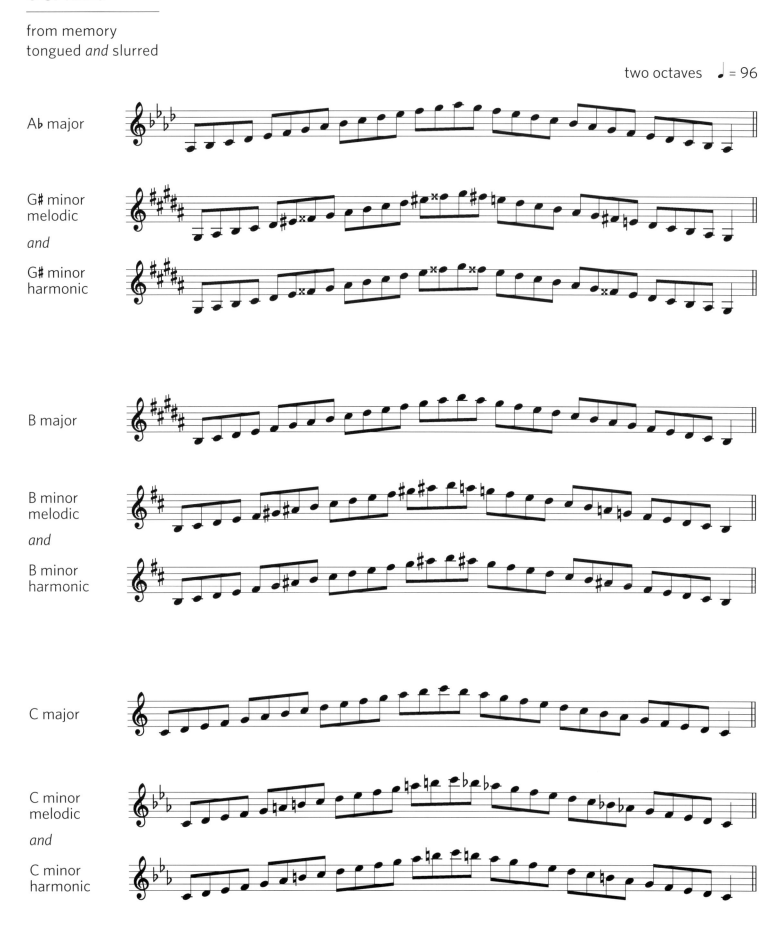

Ab major

G# minor melodic

and

G# minor harmonic

B major

B minor melodic

and

B minor harmonic

C major

C minor melodic

and

C minor harmonic

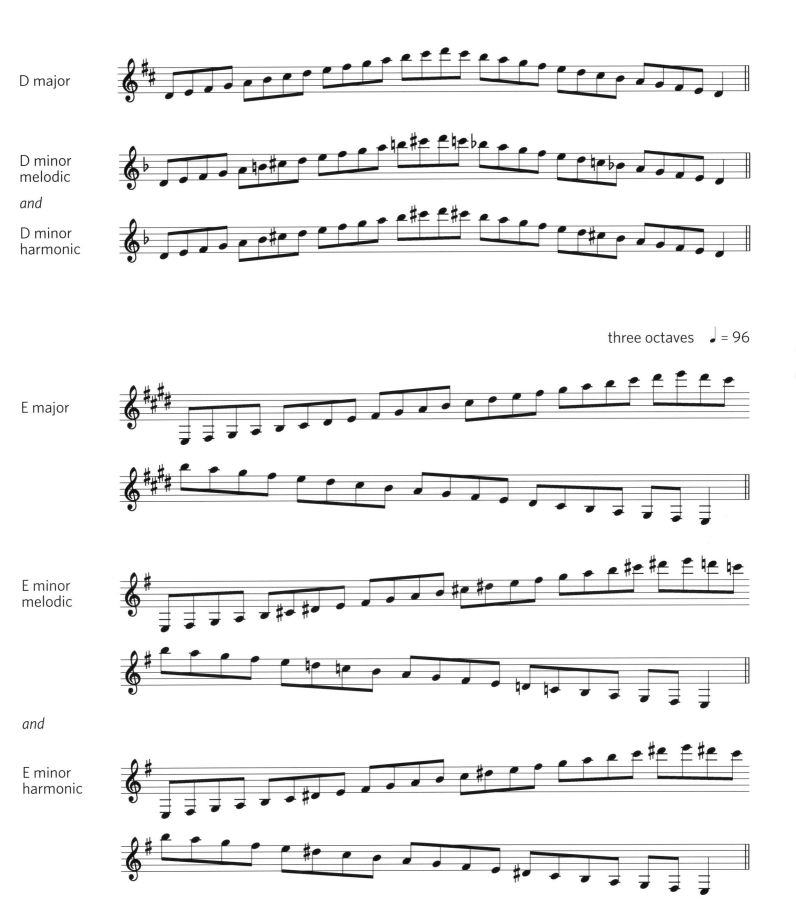

D major

D minor
melodic

and

D minor
harmonic

three octaves ♩ = 96

E major

E minor
melodic

and

E minor
harmonic

Grade 6

SCALE IN THIRDS

from memory
tongued *and* slurred

one octave ♩ = 88

Bb major

ARPEGGIOS

from memory
tongued *and* slurred

Grade 6

DOMINANT SEVENTHS

from memory
resolving on the tonic
tongued *and* slurred

two octaves ♩ = 72

in the
key of C♯

in the
key of G

three octaves ♩ = 72

in the
key of A

DIMINISHED SEVENTHS

from memory
tongued *and* slurred

two octaves ♩ = 72

starting
on G♯

starting
on D

three octaves ♩ = 72

starting
on E

For practical purposes, the diminished sevenths are notated using some enharmonic equivalents.

CHROMATIC SCALES

from memory
tongued *and* slurred

two octaves   ♩ = 96

starting
on G#

starting
on D

three octaves   ♩ = 96

starting
on E

Grade 7

SCALES

from memory
legato-tongued, staccato *and* slurred

two octaves ♩ = 112

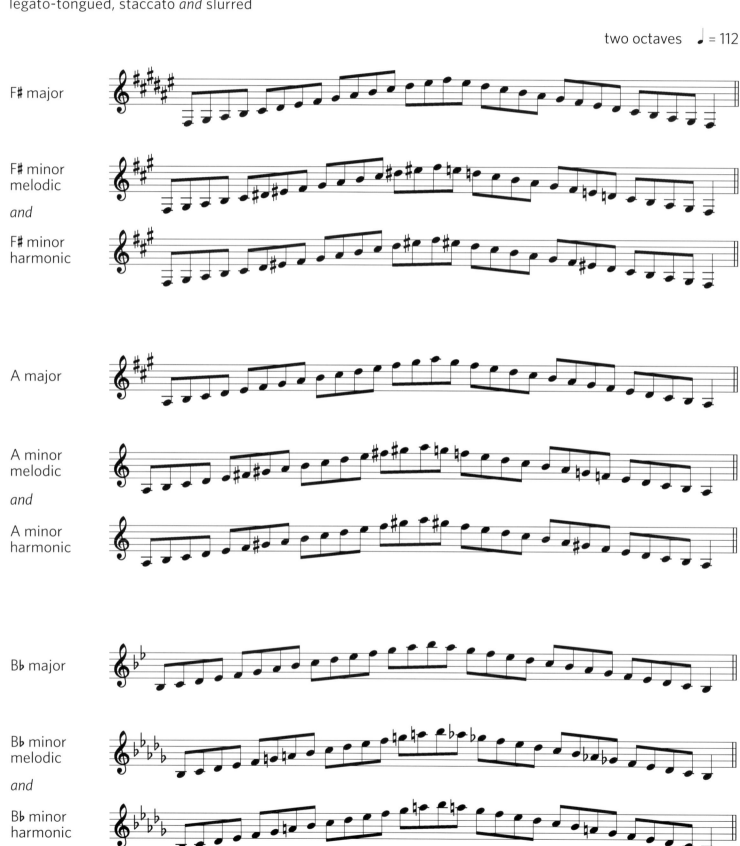

F♯ major

F♯ minor melodic

and

F♯ minor harmonic

A major

A minor melodic

and

A minor harmonic

B♭ major

B♭ minor melodic

and

B♭ minor harmonic

Grade 7

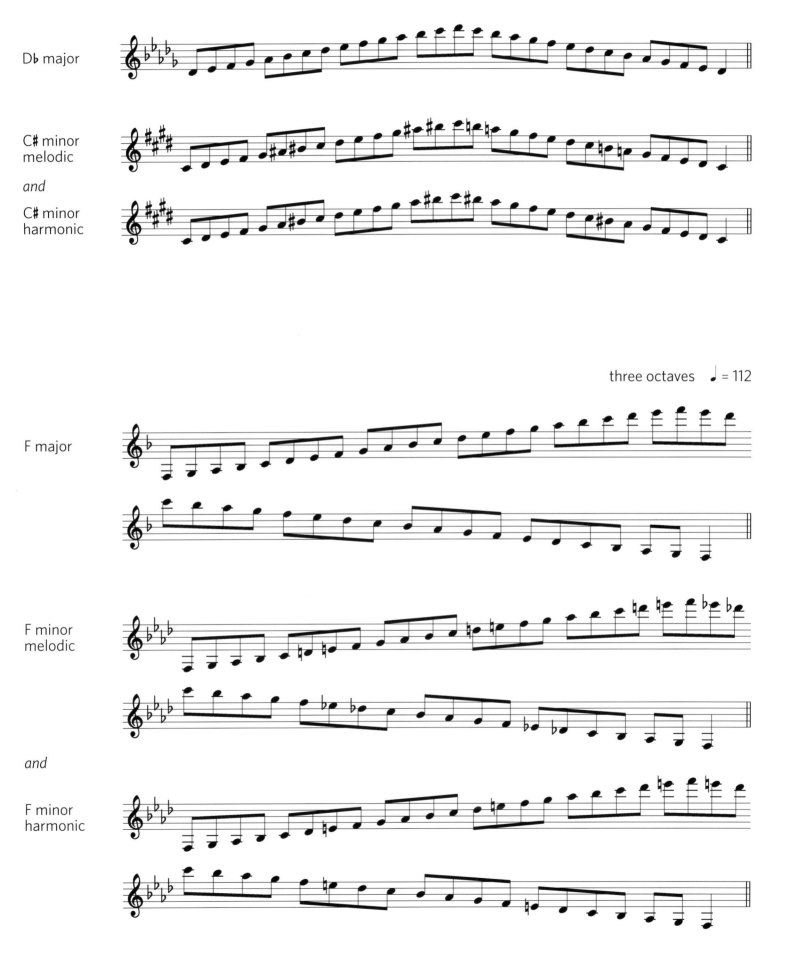

Db major

C# minor
melodic

and

C# minor
harmonic

three octaves   ♩ = 112

F major

F minor
melodic

and

F minor
harmonic

Grade 7

EXTENDED-RANGE SCALE

from memory
legato-tongued, staccato *and* slurred

♩ = 112

C major

SCALE IN THIRDS

from memory
legato-tongued, staccato *and* slurred

two octaves   ♩ = 100

G major

ARPEGGIOS

from memory
legato-tongued, staccato *and* slurred

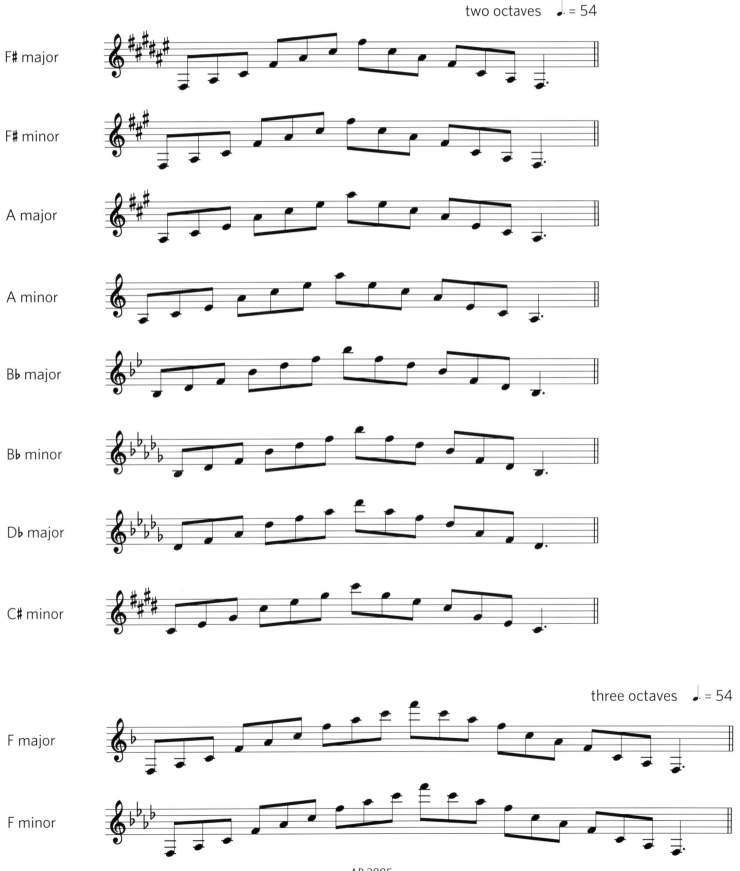

Grade 7

DOMINANT SEVENTHS

from memory
resolving on the tonic
legato-tongued, staccato *and* slurred

two octaves ♩ = 80

in the
key of B

in the
key of E♭

in the
key of F♯

three octaves ♩ = 80

in the
key of B♭

DIMINISHED SEVENTHS

from memory
legato-tongued, staccato *and* slurred

two octaves ♩ = 80

starting
on F♯

starting
on B♭

starting
on C♯

three octaves ♩ = 80

starting
on F

For practical purposes, the diminished sevenths are notated using some enharmonic equivalents.

CHROMATIC SCALES

from memory
legato-tongued, staccato *and* slurred

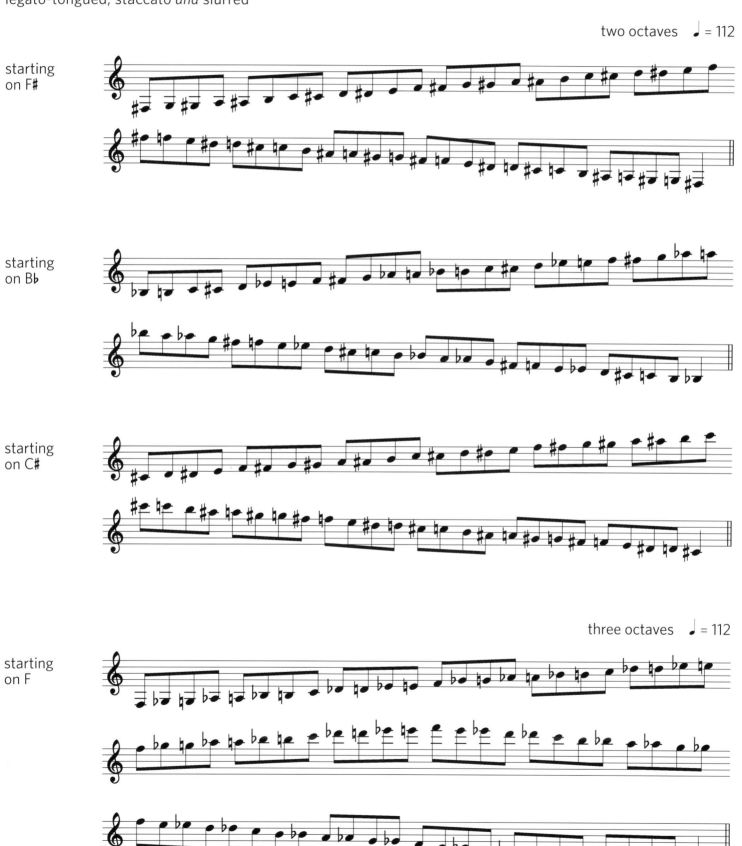

Grade 8

SCALES

from memory
legato-tongued, staccato *and* slurred

two octaves ♩ = 132

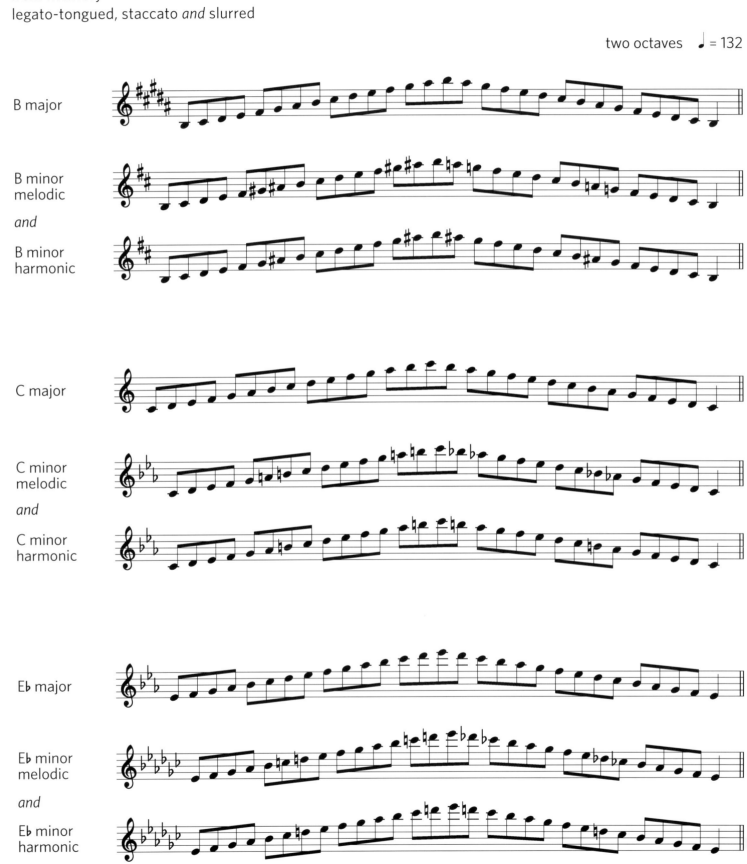

B major

B minor
melodic

and

B minor
harmonic

C major

C minor
melodic

and

C minor
harmonic

E♭ major

E♭ minor
melodic

and

E♭ minor
harmonic

Grade 8

three octaves ♩ = 132

F# major

F# minor
melodic

and

F# minor
harmonic

Grade 8

from memory
legato-tongued, staccato *and* slurred

three octaves ♩ = 132

G major

G minor
melodic

and

G minor
harmonic

Grade 8

EXTENDED-RANGE SCALES

from memory
legato-tongued, staccato *and* slurred

♩ = 132

A major

E minor
harmonic

SCALES IN THIRDS

from memory
legato-tongued, staccato *and* slurred

two octaves ♩ = 120

D major

three octaves ♩ = 120

F major

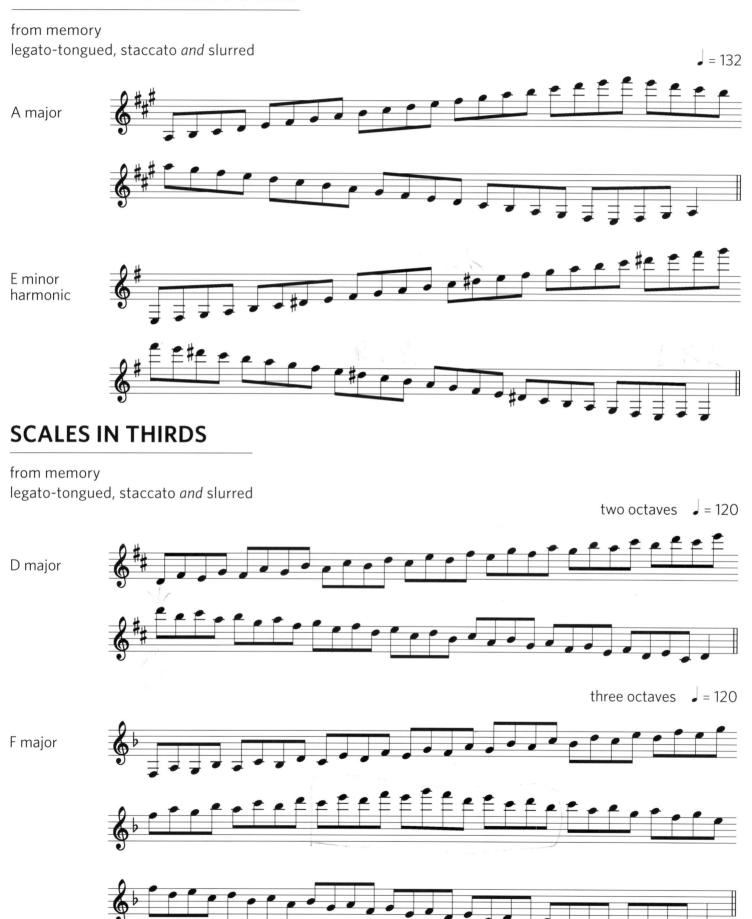

Grade 8

ARPEGGIOS

from memory
legato-tongued, staccato *and* slurred

EXTENDED-RANGE ARPEGGIOS

from memory
legato-tongued, staccato *and* slurred

$\quad$ = 96

A major

E minor

Grade 8

DOMINANT SEVENTHS

from memory
resolving on the tonic
legato-tongued, staccato *and* slurred

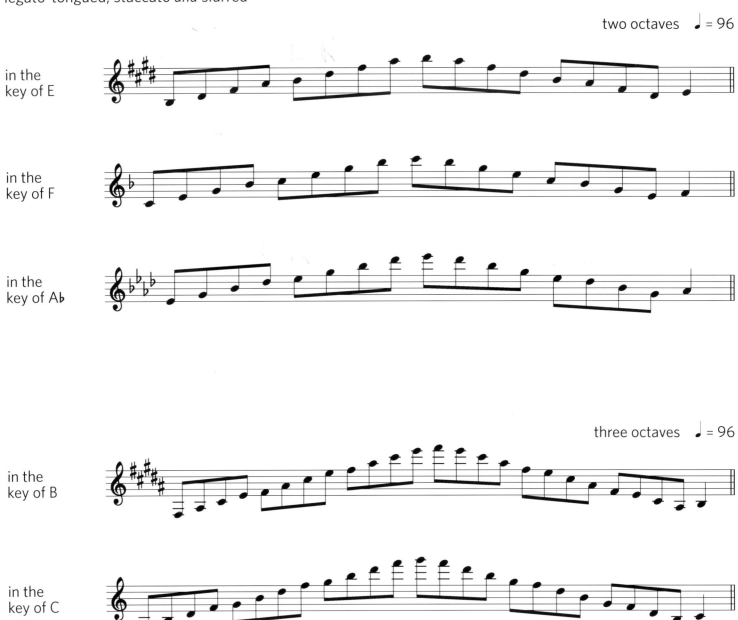

DIMINISHED SEVENTHS

from memory
legato-tongued, staccato *and* slurred

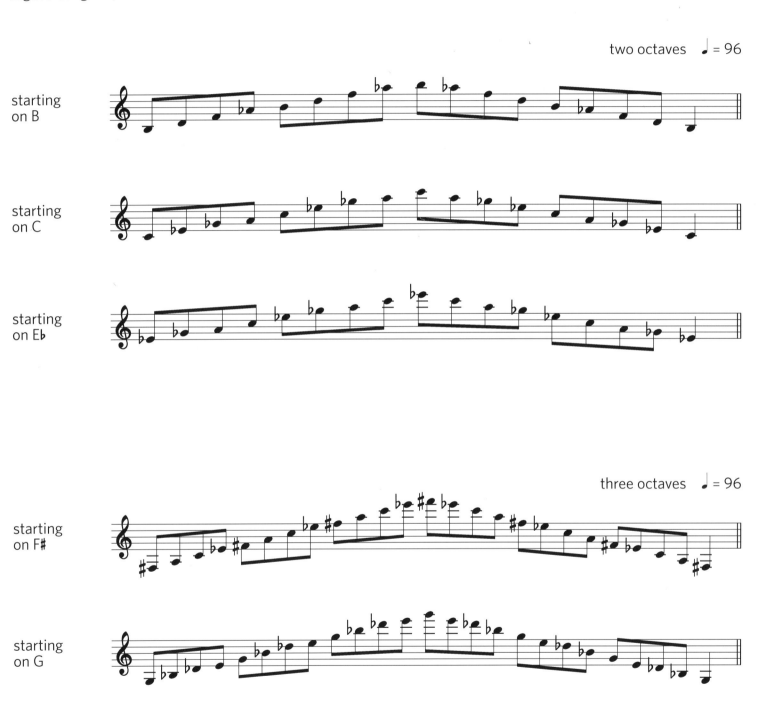

For practical purposes, the diminished sevenths are notated using some enharmonic equivalents.

Grade 8

CHROMATIC SCALES

from memory
legato-tongued, staccato *and* slurred

two octaves   ♩ = 132

starting on B

starting on C

starting on E♭

three octaves ♩ = 132

starting
on F#

starting
on G

24

Grade 8

WHOLE-TONE SCALES

from memory
legato-tongued, staccato *and* slurred

two octaves   ♩ = 132

three octaves   ♩ = 132